# Bunny Days

tao nyeu

Dial Books for Young Readers

an imprint of Penguin Group (USA) Inc.

DIAL BOOKS FOR YOUNG READERS
A division of Penguin Young Readers Group
Published by The Penguin Group • Penguin Group (USA) Inc., 375
Hudson Street, New York, NY 10014, U.S.A. • Penguin Group (Canada),
90 Eglinton Avenue East, Suite 700, Toronto, Ontario, Canada M4P 2Y3
(a division of Pearson Penguin Canada Inc.) • Penguin Books Ltd, 80
Strand, London WC2R 0RL, England • Penguin Ireland, 25 St. Stephen's
Green, Dublin 2, Ireland (a division of Penguin Books Ltd) • Penguin
Group (Australia), 250 Camberwell Road, Camberwell, Victoria 3124,
Australia (a division of Pearson Australia Group Pty Ltd) • Penguin
Books India Pvt Ltd, 11 Community Centre, Panchsheel Park, New
Delhi - 110 017, India • Penguin Group (NZ), 67 Apollo Drive, Rosedale,
North Shore 0632, New Zealand (a division of Pearson New Zealand
Ltd) • Penguin Books (South Africa) (Pty) Ltd, 24 Sturdee Avenue,
Rosebank, Johannesburg 2196, South Africa • Penguin Books Ltd,
Registered Offices: 80 Strand, London WC2R 0RL, England

The publisher does not have any control over and does not assume any
responsibility for author or third-party websites or their content.
Designed by Lily Malcom
Manufactured in China on acid-free paper

10 9 8 7 6 5 4 3 2 1

Library of Congress Cataloging-in-Publication Data

Nyeu, Tao.
  Bunny days / Tao Nyeu.
    p. cm.
  Summary: As a pair of busy goats inadvertently cause trouble for six
bunnies, their neighbor Bear comes to the rescue.
  ISBN 978-0-8037-3330-5 (hardcover)
  [1. Rabbits—Fiction. 2. Animals—Infancy—Fiction. 3. Goats—Fiction.
4. Bears—Fiction.] I. Title.
  PZ7.N992Bun 2010
  [E]—dc22
                        2009023060

The artwork was silkscreened using water-based ink.

to noah

# Contents

Muddy Bunnies * 7

Dusty Bunnies * 21

Bunny Tails * 35

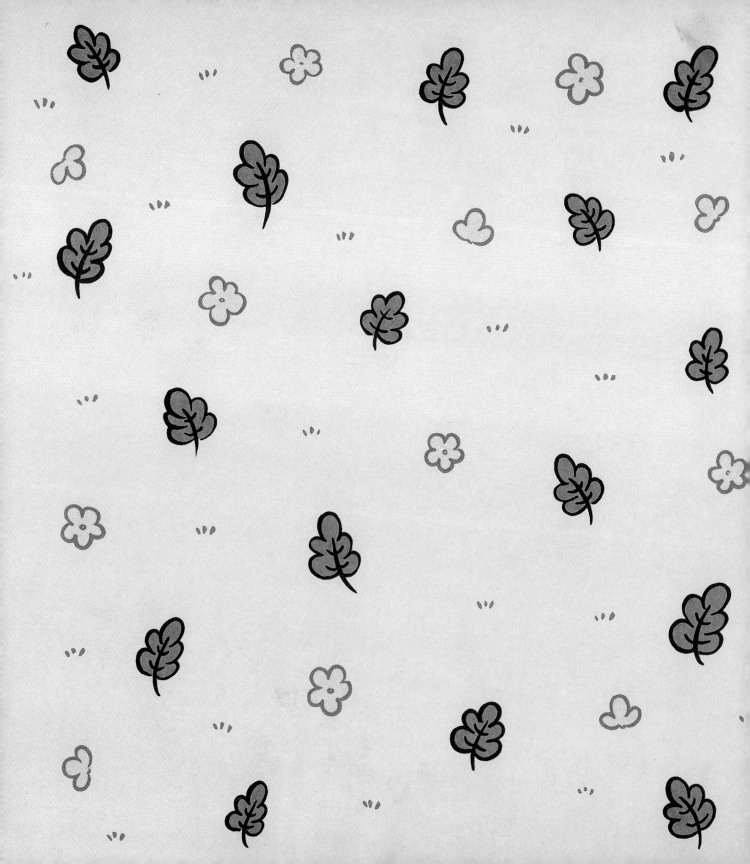

# MUDDY BUNNIES

The bunnies are soaking up the sun
when Mr. Goat drives along in his tractor.

What a mess!

They need some help from Bear.

Bear decides to use the delicate cycle.

And after a refreshing line dry all day . . .

and all night . . .

the bunnies are ready for a brand-new adventure.

Everyone is happy.

# The bunnies are dozing deep underground

as Mrs. Goat goes
about her chores.

RRRRR!

What a bother! The vacuum is broken again.

Mrs. Goat needs
Bear's help.

Achoo! This looks like a job for the big fan.

**WHIRRRRR** goes the fan.

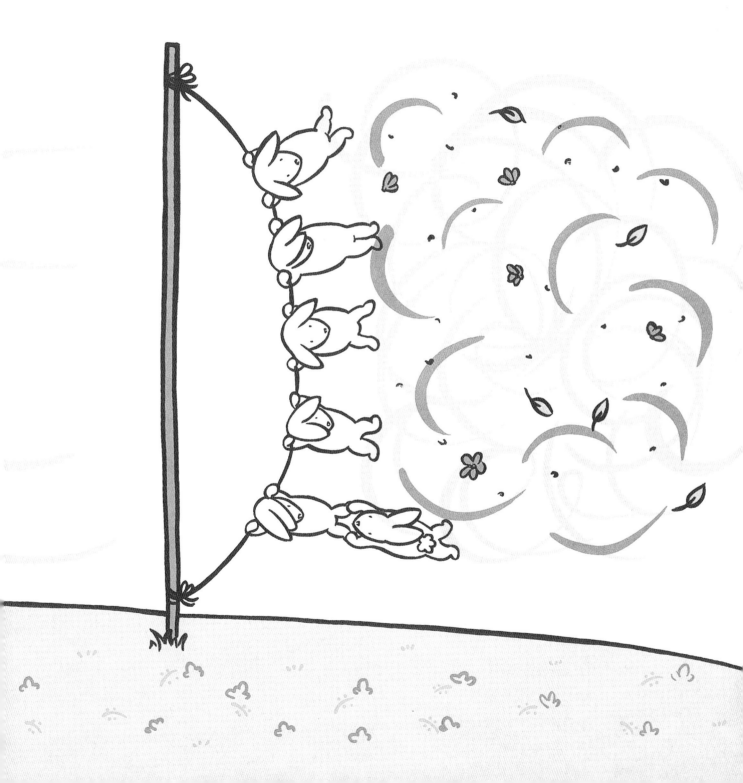

**After a few finishing touches**

and careful repairs . . .

Mrs. Goat can return to her work.
Everyone is happy.

The bunnies are playing hide-and-seek

while Mr. Goat tends to his garden.

Oh dear!

Now there are bunnies without tails
and tails without bunnies.

It's back to Bear for more help.

Bear knows just what to do.

Zumm-Zumm-Zumm-Zumm
goes the sewing machine.
Stitch by stitch,
Bear is very gentle.

And after a little bit of bed rest . . .

the bunnies are
good as new.

Everyone is happy.